MY ADVENTURE

WITH

DISNEY'S

WINNIE THE POOH

This book was especially written for
Halley Roosa
With love from
Dad and Rene

Adapted by Wendy Elks

ISBN 1 875676 16 3

There was a place near to where Halley Roosa lived at 194 Spillway Road in West Hurley called the Hundred-Acre Wood. She often played there with Paulie, Jane and Kelsey.

One day, when they were playing, Halley came across her two friends Pooh and Piglet. They were both fast asleep and since it looked as though it was going to rain, Halley gently woke them.

'Wake up, Piglet, wake up, Pooh,' she said. 'If you stay out here you'll get wet.'

Piglet blinked his eyes and sat up. Pooh yawned and stretched.

'Hello, Halley! Have you come to play?' asked Pooh.

'Yes, I'm here with Paulie, Jane and Kelsey,' answered Halley. 'But it looks as if it's going to rain.'

'Would you like to come to my house?' asked Piglet.

'Yes, but we'd better hurry. I don't want to get wet!' said Halley.

They set off. The wind was growing
stronger and stronger. It blew so hard that
Piglet, who was a very small animal, was
blown right up into the air! Luckily, Halley
caught him.

'I think I'd better carry you, Piglet,' said
Halley, 'or you might blow away again!'

'Bother!' said Pooh. 'It's starting to rain.
A big drop fell on my nose! Think. Think.
Think. Oh! My house is around the corner.
Perhaps we should go there instead of Piglet's?'

'Okay. It looks as though Paulie, Jane and
Kelsey have gone to find shelter, too,' said
Halley.

They got to Pooh's house just in time. The rain was beginning to pour down as Pooh shut the door.

'Well, that's the end of the Honey Expedition,' he said gloomily.

'What's a Honey Expedition?' asked Halley.

'A search for honey,' explained Pooh. 'Winter is coming, and bears don't go out much in the winter. So, seeing as I'm a bear, and I love honey, I thought I'd better build up my supply. Piglet and I have been searching for honey all day.'

'We got tired. We sat down to rest, and fell asleep,' added Piglet.

'I'll help you search some more when it stops raining,' offered Halley.

'Oh, thank you, Halley!' said Pooh. He yawned. 'It's getting late. I think I'll go to bed now and wait for the rain to stop.'

So Pooh went to bed, and Halley and Piglet read a book together.

The rain was falling softly outside. It was so quiet and peaceful that Halley and Piglet fell asleep too. The next morning they woke up to the sound of Pooh crying out, 'Oh! Oh! My house is leaking!'

Halley squealed when she realized that Pooh's house was filling up with water!

'The water has washed all my honey pots clean. Now I have no honey at all,' Pooh said sadly.

Halley waded to the window. 'There are flood waters all around the house, Pooh,' she said. 'We'll have to try to reach higher ground.'

Pooh climbed out the window onto a branch. 'Don't let my honey pots float away, or I won't have anything to keep my honey in!' he cried.

'I think we should all float out of here ourselves,' said Halley.

Soon they were floating down the stream. Pooh had a chair for a boat. Halley was floating on an upside-down table, and little Piglet was bobbing in one of the empty honey jars.

After a while, they floated right up to Christopher Robin and some of their other friends who were standing on dry ground.

'Hello, Pooh! Hello, Piglet! Hello, Halley!' called Christopher Robin. 'What are you doing floating around like that?'

'There was a flood in my house, and all my honey has gone,' explained Pooh. 'And I have a rumbly in my tumbly.'

'We need to find him some honey now!' added Halley.

'Oh, poor Pooh! Well, I think I know of a tree with honey in it,' said Christopher Robin. 'Let's go!' They walked through the wood until they came to a very tall tree. Way up high there was a hole in the trunk, with bees buzzing around it.

'It's a long way up, Pooh,' said Halley. 'Can you climb that high?'

'If there's honey up that high, I can climb up that high,' said Pooh. And up he went.

'Oh dear,' he said when he was a long way up. 'My paws are getting tired.'

All of a sudden Pooh was on his way down the tree. 'Oh bother! I wish it was as fast as this on the way up,' he thought to himself as he bounced from branch to branch. He landed on the ground with a thud.

'Don't try again, Pooh. It's too dangerous,' said Halley. 'We'll find honey somewhere else.'

But Pooh was not the sort to give up easily — especially when he put his mind to honey.

This time Pooh climbed all the way up. He had to wriggle out onto a very thin branch to reach the hole. And just as he did, the branch went SNAP! and down he went again.

'Silly Ol' Bear,' said Christopher Robin. 'You can't reach the hole now with that branch broken, Pooh.'

'Oh, yes I can,' said Pooh, who was a very determined bear. 'Would you, by any chance, have a balloon, Christopher Robin?'

'Yes,' said Christopher Robin. 'But what do you want a balloon for?'

'Honey!' whispered Pooh, 'you'll see.'

Christopher Robin and Halley ran off to get a balloon. Pooh grabbed hold of the balloon's string and started floating up into the air. Halley took his feet and guided him towards the honeybee's hive.

'Oh, thank you, Halley,' called Pooh as he floated up. The bees swarmed angrily around Pooh when he stuck his paw in the hole. Then the string came loose on the balloon. The air came out with a whoosh!

'Oh, dear!' cried Pooh. He held on tight as the balloon sped along, with hundreds of bees swarming after him.

When Pooh finally came back to earth, he found that he was right near Rabbit's house.

'Oh, wonderful! Rabbit always has honey!' thought Pooh happily.

Halley, Christopher Robin and the others caught up to Pooh.

RABBIT'S HOWSE

Rabbit looked rather worried, as though he knew what Pooh was thinking about.

'Ah, Pooh Bear,' said Rabbit rather uncertainly. 'Ah, how about some lunch?'

'Thank you, Rabbit. Perhaps just a small smackerel of honey,' said Pooh.

Pooh squeezed through Rabbit's front door behind Rabbit.

'People can't fit through Rabbit's front door,' explained Christopher Robin. 'We'll have to wait out here. We may as well sit down — this could take a while!' he added.

Meanwhile, Halley told Christopher Robin about her last birthday which was on March 28th. Paulie, Jane and Kelsey had decorated her home at 194 Spillway Road, West Hurley with lots of balloons of different shapes and colors. They had had so much fun playing games and eating all the delicious cakes!

Inside, Rabbit watched as Pooh ate and ate and ate.

Rabbit shook his head. 'Will you be staying long?' he asked Pooh. Pooh looked at the honey jars. There was only one left.

'Not very long,' he said.

RABBIT'Z
HOWSE

When he had finished, Pooh tried to wiggle through Rabbit's front door. When he was halfway in and halfway out, he stopped. 'This door hole seems to have shrunk,' he said.

'Er, I think it might be you who has grown bigger, Pooh,' said Halley.

Pooh had eaten so much honey that he was bigger than ever before. He was stuck!

'Everybody, pull!' cried Christopher Robin. All the friends got into a line and pulled. But it was no use. Pooh didn't budge.

'Poor Pooh,' said Christopher Robin. 'I think we'll have to wait for Pooh to get thinner.'

And so they did.

And then one morning when Rabbit was beginning to think that he might never be able to use his front door again, it happened.

'He budged!' cried Rabbit. 'Christopher Robin! He bidged. He badged. He boodged!'

'Heave ho! Heave ho!' shouted all the friends. They tugged on Pooh outside as Rabbit pushed from the inside.

Rabbit pushed, and Halley, Christopher Robin and the others pulled with all their might. Suddenly there was a loud POP! Halley fell back onto Christopher Robin, and Christopher Robin fell back onto poor Kanga and Eeyore rolled away into the bushes.

Pooh had shot out of Rabbit's front door like a rocket.

'There he goes!' cried Rabbit.

'Uh oh,' said Halley, shading her eyes to watch. 'Pooh is headed right for that old tree trunk. Watch out, Pooh!'

Everyone watched as Pooh's head and shoulders disappeared into a hole in the tree trunk, like a cork into a bottle.

'Pooh!' shouted Christopher Robin. 'Are you all right?'

'Oh yes! I'm the happiest bear in the world!' sang Pooh! 'I've just discovered the biggest supply of honey I've ever seen! And the bees have gone and left it all to me! Thank you, Halley!'

'You're welcome Pooh,' said Halley. 'Let's go and get your honey pots so that we can fill them all up. Then you'll have a supply of honey for the whole winter.'

'Uh, do you think you could get them for me?' asked Pooh. 'I think I'd better stay here and mind the honey.'

Laughing together, Halley and her friends set off for Pooh's house.

BOOK
No. 20
▶

BOOK
No. 19
▶

BOOK
No. 16
▶

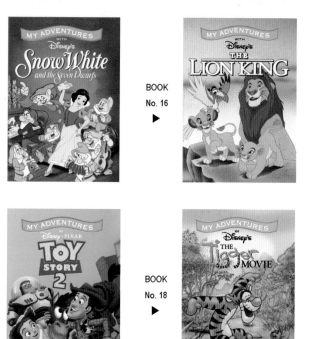

QUALITY
CONTROL
RECORD

BOOK
No. 17
▶

BOOK
No. 18
▶

We have used the following information provided to produce your Personalized Book.
IMPORTANT - Additional books ordered will be mailed to you separately - please
allow a few days for differences in delivery times.

This book was ordered by:

R ROOSA
12 EDNSONS CT
CHICOPEE MA 01020

This book was specially printed for:

FIRST NAME	Halley
LAST NAME	Roosa
ADDRESS	194 Spillway Road
	West Hurley NY
DATE OF BIRTH	03/28/91
FRIEND	Paulie
FRIEND	Jane
FRIEND	Kelsey
BOOKPLATE	Dad and Rene

My Adventures with
Disney's
Winnie the Pooh
649/261001/29717/13 122/23

4 00649 30001 3

**This is Your
Account Number**

TO ORDER MORE BOOKS

My Adventure Books
PO Box 9203
Central Islip NY 11722-9203
Phone: (631) 851 5295